P9-DTU-555

TigerWoman

WRITTEN BY LAURENCE YEP
PICTURES BY ROBERT ROTH

BridgeWater Books

Text copyright © 1995 by Laurence Yep.
Illustrations copyright © 1995 by Robert Roth.
Calligraphy by Barbara Bash.
Designed by Leslie Bauman.
Published by BridgeWater Books, an imprint of Troll Associates, Inc.
Printed in Mexico.
10 9 8 7 6 5 4 3 2

Library of Congress Cataloging-in-Publication
Yep, Laurence.
Tiger woman / by Laurence Yep; pictures by Robert Roth.
p. cm.
Summary: When she refuses to share her food with a beggar, an old
woman finds herself transformed into various animals, until she
learns a lesson about greed.
ISBN 0-8167-3464-X
[1. Folklore—China.]   I. Roth, Robert, 1965–   ill.   II. Title.
PZ8.1.Y37Ti   1995   398.2—dc20   [E]   93-38685

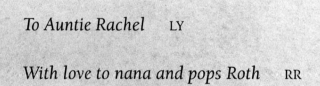

To Auntie Rachel LY

With love to nana and pops Roth RR

There once was a selfish old woman who would never share anything. Her favorite food was bean curd, which she made in smooth, white, glistening sheets and cut into little cubes. Then she would steam it or boil it or fry it. On hot days, she would eat it cold with a little soy sauce and scallions.

On market days she ate her bean curd and rice on her doorstep so she could watch the spectacle. Farmers and shepherds and goatherds, sellers of birds and sellers of crickets, portrait painters and toy peddlers—all of them came to the square. Even the rich folk visited, carried in sedan chairs on the shoulders of sweaty men.

One market day as the woman stuffed herself, she watched her neighbor bargain with a farmer for a scoopful of grain. Just as she finished her meal, a ragged old man limped into town and saw her. He bowed and said,

"Your bean curd gleams like the whitest jade.
I'm so empty. Please come to my aid."

The old woman glared and said,

"A sillier thing I've never heard.
I will not waste my sweet bean curd."

The beggar shook his head.

"If you let your belly rule you,
it will surely trick and fool you."

The old woman replied,

"I'm a tiger when I'm famished.
So begone, old beggar, vanish!"

And she poked him with her chopsticks to drive him away.

The old man waved his staff solemnly and said,

"By wind and rain. By moon and star!
You will be what you say you are!"

And then he limped away.

Between sips of tea, the woman ate her last cube of bean curd. Right away, her skin began to itch. But when she tried to scratch, all she felt was fur. Puzzled, she looked and saw that her hands had turned to paws.

Her neighbor pointed in her direction and said to the farmer,

> "I think my eyes are tricking me.
> Is that a tiger roaming free
> with claws so smooth they almost shine?
> Has it come to town to dine?"

Frightened, the old woman dropped her cup of tea, and began looking around frantically for the savage beast.

When the farmer saw her, the scoop fell from his hand, scattering grain all over. He shouted,

"That tiger's hunting for a treat.
And you and I look much too sweet!"

Then the two men ran for their lives.
The old woman looked down at her reflection in the spilled tea.

"Who's that I see there in the tea?
It's got my dress. The tiger's me!"

Far down the street she saw the sunlight wink off the spear tips of many soldiers.

Terrified, she ran into her house, but the soldiers pursued her.

The captain waved his sword and shouted,

*"A prize to the one who takes her head.
I'll hang that head above my bed."*

As the soldiers closed in, the old woman desperately leapt out a window and hid inside a sedan chair. On the seat she found half a piece of steamed bread that a chair bearer had been eating before he ran away from the tiger.

*"I'd be a dumb ox to waste a snack.
His bread won't be here when he comes back."*

Before anyone else could eat it, she greedily chomped it down.

Instantly, her claws fused together and
became hooves.

The sedan chair suddenly felt very tight—
until she grew so big that the sides of the chair
split and she wore the curtains on her ears.

As the soldiers poured out of her house, they
pointed their spears at her and shouted,

"Get a box. Get a noose!
There's an ox out on the loose!"

Trying to escape, the old woman galloped into the tailor's stall. Out she burst, wrapped in long sheets of dyed silk. Then she dodged through the portrait painter's booth and became a rainbow of different-colored inks. Round and round the market she went, smashing carts and knocking over stalls. Birds and crickets flew from their broken cages. Goats broke their halters and butted the soldiers.

Finally, the soldiers threw ropes around her neck and legs and even on her tail. As an angry crowd gathered in the ruined square, the captain announced,

*"Since this ox has wrecked each store,
its steaks must settle up the score."*

The old woman bellowed,

*"But that would be a big mistake.
You're sure to get a bellyache."*

Everyone ignored her. As the soldiers went to find the butcher, the old woman saw some grain on the ground. For a moment her greed made her forget her fear.

*"Even a dumb bird would eat this grain.
The farmer's loss will be my gain."*

Hurriedly, she gobbled up the grain before anyone else could find it. In the wink of an eye, she began to shrink, and the ropes plopped to the dirt. In a bronze mirror lying on the ground, she saw that she was now a little sparrow.

With a flap of her wings, she rose into the air, swept around the market, and soared over a high wall into a garden where willow trees stood beside a lake. A green pavilion thrust out onto the water like a giant lily pad. There, a rich man fed some birds.

"So this is how the rich folk live.
I'll hide here as a fugitive.
My refuge will be elegant.
But I'm as starved as an elephant."

Landing among the birds, she began to peck at a sesame seed. When the other birds complained, she chased them away. Soon she had gobbled up all the seeds on the ground.

As soon as she had swallowed the last seed, she swelled up so fast that she knocked the surprised man into the water. He spluttered and cried,

"The doors are locked and the gates are barred.
How did an elephant enter my yard?"

She tried to escape as the servants answered their master's calls for help. Wearing the pavilion roof like a hat, she headed for the nearest doorway. But she was so big, she got stuck. With a lunge, she pulled down the doorway, and with it, the whole side of the pavilion.

In a panic, she blundered through the mansion seeking someplace to hide. She tried to crawl under a big four-poster bed, but the servants found her. She tried to squeeze inside a wardrobe, but smashed it into kindling. She tried to climb a set of shelves, but only wrecked a collection of prize perfume bottles.

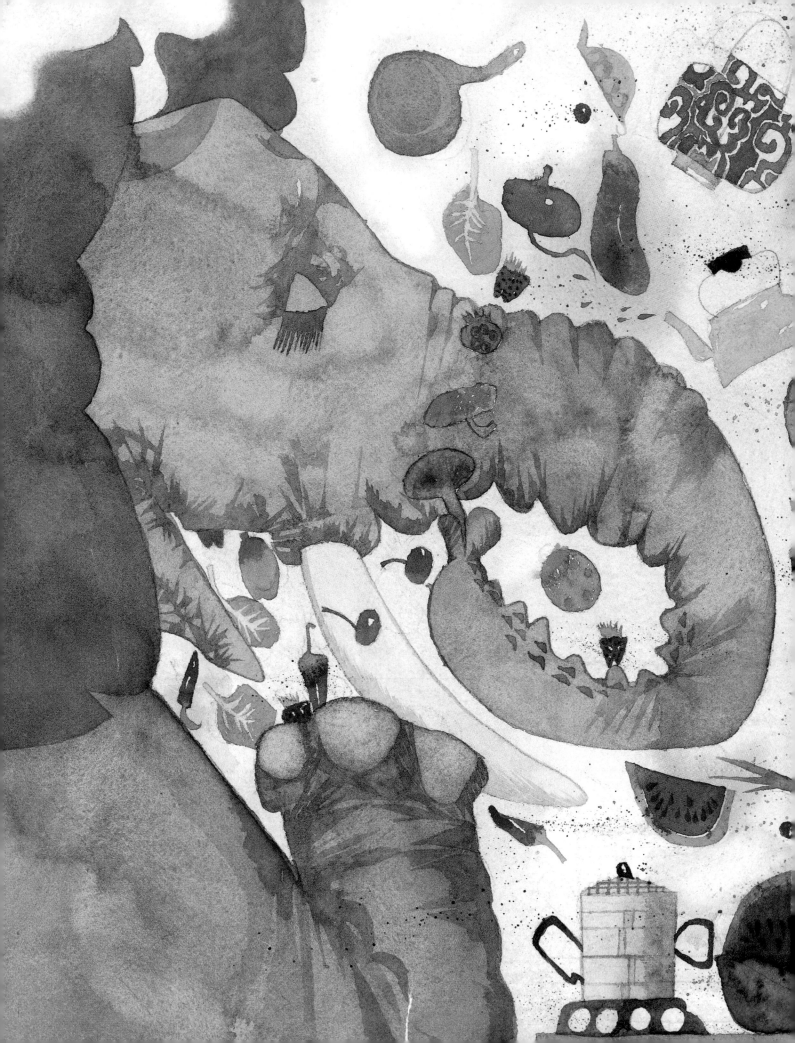

Finally, she wound up in the kitchen, where the cook was chopping vegetables and slicing meat. Flapping her elephant ears, she looked around.

"I've worked up such an appetite
that I must take one teensy bite.
But why stop there? I'll be a swine.
I'll eat your food and drink your wine."

As fast as her trunk could move, she crammed food into her mouth. Bowls smashed and knives and spoons fell from the table.

When she had finished everything in sight, she began to shrink again. Looking at her reflection in the blade of a shiny cleaver, she saw that she had become a pig.

A hand grabbed her hind leg.

> *"Since you've devoured my lovely feast,*
> *you'll take its place, you horrid beast."*

And the cook tied her to a table.

As she listened to the cook sharpen his cleaver, the old woman gazed at a glistening cube of bean curd that had fallen to the floor near her. Once again she remembered the old beggar and his curse. She grunted sadly,

> *"If I had fed that poor old man,*
> *I would not end up in a pan.*
> *Why was I mean? Why didn't I share?*
> *He could've had half. It would've been fair."*

Since this was going to be her last meal, she nibbled sadly at the bean curd until it was gone.

The next moment she changed back into a human. The cook stared at her in shock.

*"Who are you, and where's my sow?
I must prepare my supper now."*

The old woman stood up and glared at the man. Then, with a shrug of her shoulders, she turned and marched straight home.

After that, beggars never went hungry if they came to her door. She served them cubes of bean curd, smooth and shiny as white jade.

As she told everyone,

"In kindness I've become a believer,
since I faced the wrong end of the cleaver."

Based on a Shantung folk song.